Jason Altman

GREAT ILLUSTRATED CLASSICS

AROUND THE WORLD IN 80 DAYS

Jules Verne

adapted by
Marian Leighton

Illustrations by
Pablo Marcos Studio

GREAT ILLUSTRATED CLASSICS

edited by
Malvina G. Vogel

visit us at
www.abdopub.com

Library edition published in 2002 by ABDO Publishing Company, 4940 Viking Drive, Suite 622, Edina, Minnesota 55435. Published by agreement with Playmore Incorporated Publishers and Waldman Publishing Corporation.

Printed in the United States.

Library of Congress Cataloging-in-Publication Data

Verne, Jules, 1828-1905.
    Around the world in 80 days / Jules Verne ; adapted by Marian Leighton ; illustrated by Pablo Marcos Studio.
        p. cm -- (Great illustrated classics)
    Reprint. Originally published: New York: Playmore: Waldman Pub., 1989.
    Summary: In 1872, English gentleman Phileas Fogg has many adventures as he tries to win a bet that he can travel around the world in eighty days.
    ISBN 1-57765-680-6
    [1. Voyages around the world--Fiction. 2. Adventure and adventurers--Fiction.] I. Title: Around the world in eighty days. II. Leighton, Marian. III. Pablo Marcos Studio.

PZ7.V594 Ar 2002
[Fic]--dc21
                                                                                2001056482

CONTENTS

CHAPTER   PAGE

About the Author

Jules Verne was born in Nantes, France. As a child, he developed a great interest in travel and exploration. He continued to display this interest throughout his life as a writer of adventure stories and science fiction. He also wrote several books on history and geography.

Verne's first book, *Five Weeks in a Balloon*, was published in 1863. It made him wealthy and famous. The following year he wrote *A Journey to the Center of the Earth*, and the year after that came *From the Earth to the Moon*.

Around the World in 80 Days appeared in 1873. Along with *20,000 Leagues Under the Sea* (published in 1870), it is probably Verne's most popular work.

Phileas Fogg, the English Gentleman

Chapter 1
Phileas Fogg Meets Passepartout

On October 2, 1872, Phileas Fogg bet his life savings that he could travel around the world in 80 days.

Mr. Fogg, an English gentleman, lived at No. 7 Saville Row in London, but not much else was known about him. He never went to the business and social places where important Londoners gathered. Nor did he hold a regular job. He seemed to be quite rich, but nobody knew where all his money came from. He spent most of his time at the Reform Club, reading in the library there and playing whist, a popular English card game. Otherwise, he kept mostly to himself.

Perhaps the most remarkable thing about Phileas Fogg was that his life centered upon the clock. His own clock told not only the hour, minute and second, but also the month and year. Fogg was never early and never late, and his activities followed the same pattern day after day.

For example, at exactly 11:30 every morning, Phileas Fogg went to the Reform Club. He ate lunch and dinner there each day at exactly the same time, in the same room, at the same table, and always alone. At exactly midnight, he returned home and went straight to bed.

Phileas Fogg had no wife, children, relatives or close friends. He shared his large house with a servant, but had just fired him for bringing shaving water that was two degrees too cold. Now he was awaiting a new

Watching the Clock as Usual

man to replace the other servant. There was a knock at the door, and a young man entered.

"You come from France and your name is John, is that right?" Fogg greeted him.

"Please call me Jean. My last name is Passepartout—a name I picked up by moving from one job to another. I have worked as a singer, a circus performer, a gym teacher and a fireman. Then, five years ago, I left France to become a household servant here in England. That job ended badly, but I hope now to settle down here with you and forget the name Passepartout."

"Good! What time is it?"

"My watch says 11:25."

"Oh," sighed Phileas Fogg, "you're four minutes slow! But never mind! Starting right now, at 11:29 on Wednesday, October 2, you are in my service."

Fogg Meets Passepartout.

"You're Hired!"

Chapter 2
A New Life for a Frenchman

Passepartout had been watching Phileas Fogg carefully during their short talk, and he liked what he saw. Fogg was a tall, good-looking man about 40 years old, with light hair and a moustache, pale skin, and beautiful teeth. He spoke and moved slowly and with perfect control of his words and actions.

As for Passepartout, he wasn't at all bad looking, although his lips were a bit too large and his hair messy. His muscles were very well developed from his days in the circus and the gym. The greatest difference between

Fogg and Passepartout, however, lay in their personalities: the master was quiet and withdrawn, while the servant was lively and talkative.

Would Passepartout be able to adjust to Fogg's orderly and regular way of life? He had not fared too well in other English households. His most recent job had ended quickly when he scolded his master, young Lord Longferry, for coming home drunk. He certainly didn't expect any such behavior from Phileas Fogg.

As soon as Mr. Fogg left for the Reform Club, Passepartout began looking around the house. How neat and clean everything was! The master's clothes and shoes even had numbers showing what time of the year they were to be worn. Passepartout walked from Fogg's bedroom to the room that he guessed would be his own. The large clock he saw there was timed to the second with that in

A New Life for Passepartout

Phileas Fogg's room. On the wall above the clock was a list of things for the servant to do. Passepartout learned from reading the list that Fogg awoke at exactly 8:00 each morning and left at exactly 11:30 for the Reform Club. Passepartout's duties would include serving his master tea and toast at 8:23, bringing his shaving water at 9:37 and helping him get dressed starting at 9:40. There would be many other chores to attend to between 11:30, when Fogg left the house, and midnight, when he went to bed.

Passepartout began to think of Phileas Fogg as some kind of machine, but he continued to look forward to his new job as a welcome change from the past.

So Much Work!

Fogg at the Reform Club

Chapter 3
Phileas Fogg Makes a Famous Bet

At exactly 11:30, Phileas Fogg set out for his daily walk to the Reform Club. His regular table was set for lunch. He finished eating at exactly 13 minutes before 1:00 and went into the library. It took him until 3:45 to read the *Times* and until dinnertime to finish the *Standard*. He finished dinner at 5:40. Half an hour later, his whist partners arrived: Andrew Stuart, an engineer; John Sullivan and Samuel Fallentin, bankers; Thomas Flanagan, a beer brewer; and Gautier Ralph, a director of the Bank of England.

A robbery had just occurred at the bank. The thief had escaped with 55,000 pounds. According to a witness, the robber was dressed like an English gentleman. The witness described him to the police, and detectives were sent all over England and to English territories overseas to catch him. A reward of 2,000 pounds had been offered for his capture.

"The robber will surely get away," said Stuart. "The world is certainly big enough to hide him."

"It was once," said Phileas Fogg, who rarely spoke during whist games. He put down his cards and declared, "Gentlemen, it is now posssible to go around the world in 80 days! From London to Suez by railroad and steamboat would take 7 days; from Suez to Bombay, India, by rail, 13 days; from Bombay to Calcutta by rail, 3 days; from Calcutta to Hong Kong by steamer, 13 days; from Hong Kong to Yokohama, Japan, by steamer, 6

A Game of Whist

days; from Japan to California by steamer, 22 days; from California to New York by rail, 7 days; and from New York back to London by steamer and rail, 9 days. Altogether, that makes 80 days!"

"That may be so," said Stuart, "but you might have bad weather, a railroad accident, a shipwreck, or an Indian attack."

"Even so, the trip could be made in 80 days. Shall we try it, Mr. Stuart?"

"No, not me! But I'll bet 4,000 pounds that it can't be done."

"I have 20,000 pounds in the bank, and I'll bet it all!" Fogg declared. "I can leave tonight. I'll take the train for Dover at 8:45. Today is Wednesday, October 2, I'll be back in this very room on Saturday, December 21, at 8:45. Otherwise, all my money is yours!"

Phileas Fogg wrote out a check for 20,000 pounds. This was half his fortune. He would need the other half for travel expensess.

Steamer and Rail Schedules

It was 7:00 by then, and Fogg's whist partners offered to put the cards away so Mr. Fogg could get ready for his trip.

"I'm ready right now," Fogg replied. "Please deal the cards, gentlemen!"

A Check for 20,000 Pounds!

"There's No Time to Lose!"

Chapter 4
A Hurried Departure

At 7:25 Phileas Fogg gathered up his winnings from whist and left the Reform Club. Imagine Passepartout's amazement when his master arrived home long before his usual midnight hour.

"We're leaving for Dover, England, and Calais, France, in ten minutes!" Fogg declared.

"Are you leaving home, sir?"

"Yes. We're going around the world—we have to be back in 80 days! There's no time to lose!"

Passepartout was speechless. Finally, he asked, "What about the suitcases?"

"There's no time to get suitcases. Just pack a bag with two shirts and three pairs of socks for each of us. Bring my coat, raincoat, and some walking shoes too. And hurry!"

The servant was flabbergasted! Surely this was a joke! Just when he was ready to settle down to a quiet life, this had to happen! However, he packed a bag as he was told. Fogg added a railroad and steamboat timetable and a large roll of banknotes to the clothes in the bag.

"Take good care of this bag," he warned. "There are 20,000 pounds in banknotes inside!"

Phileas Fogg and Passepartout hailed a taxi and reached the railroad station at 8:20. A beggar woman holding a baby approached them for money. Fogg gave her everything that he had just won at whist. Master and

Passepartout Packs a Bag.

servant then bought first-class tickets for France. The train pulled out at exactly 8:45. Suddenly, Passepartout cried out, "Master, in my hurry I forgot to turn off the gas burner in my room!"

"Very well, young man," Fogg replied. "Your gas bill will be awaiting you when we return."

A Generous Man

Phileas Fogg Bonds for Sale!

Chapter 5
England Bets on Fogg

News of Phileas Fogg's wager spread like wildfire all over England, and it was printed in all the newspapers. The English, who love to place bets, gambled on Fogg's chances to make the trip in 80 days. Some thought it could indeed be done, but most believed Fogg was crazy and had been conned by his "friends" at the Reform Club.

So-called "Phileas Fogg bonds" were sold everywhere—but their value fell sharply with the rumor that Fogg was the gentleman who had robbed the Bank of England.

It was a certain Detective Fix who "discovered" Phileas Fogg's true identity. The London police chief sent him to Suez, in Egypt, to look for the robber and promised to send an arrest warrant after him. Egypt was then part of the British Empire, and the Suez Canal had been built as a short cut for ships traveling between England and India, which was also part of the Empire.

When they heard the rumors that Fogg was the bank robber, people suddenly recalled his strange habits and his desire to be alone most of the time. They viewed his around-the-world trip as an excuse for him to leave London before the police could arrest him. Why else would he lay a large sum like 20,000 pounds on the line?

Setting Sail for Suez

Detective Fix Awaits Fogg.

Chapter 6
Detective Fix Trails a "Bank Robber"

At 11:00 on October 9, the English steamer *Mongolia* was due in Suez. Detective Fix waited nervously on the deck.

"How will you recognize the robber even if he's on board?" asked the English consul, or government representative. "From the way the London police describe him, he looks like an honest man."

"Don't worry, consul. I've arrested plenty of robbers. I'll know this one if I see him. He won't get away!"

"I hope you're right, Mr. Fix!"

"The robber would be foolish to travel on to India, wouldn't he?" Fix asked.

"Maybe not," replied the consul. "If he's smart, he'll go to India because he knows the police wouldn't expect him to!"

The *Mongolia* arrived right on time. One of the passengers approached Fix to ask where the consul's office was. The consul was supposed to stamp his passport, or travel book, with a visa to show that he had stopped at Suez.

Fix looked at the passport. Inside was a picture that matched exactly the description of the London bank robber!

"Is this your passport?" the detective asked.

"No, it belongs to my master."

"He must appear before the consul in person in order to get a visa," said Fix.

Fix Looks at the Passport.

"Don't Give Him a Visa."

Chapter 7
A Visit to Suez

"I think I've got my man!" shouted Fix, bursting into the consul's office.

"That may be so, Mr. Fix, but I don't think he'll come to see me. A robber just doesn't let people know where he is. Besides, the passport doesn't really need to be stamped with a visa at Suez."

"If he comes, don't give him a visa," begged Fix, hoping to keep the robber in Suez until the arrest warrant arrived.

"I can't refuse the visa," said the consul. "Arresting him is your problem, not mine."

A knock sounded, and a man entered the room to request a visa.

"Are you Phileas Fogg?" asked the consul, eyeing the passport.

"Yes, sir."

"And who is this man?"

"My servant, Passepartout."

"Where are you going?"

"To Bombay, India."

"You don't need a visa."

"I know that, but I want to prove that I passed through Suez."

The consul stamped the passport, never guessing that Fogg needed the visa to prove to his friends that he had won his bet honestly.

Phileas Fogg returned to the steamer and took out his diary. He noted his arrival in Suez after traveling through England, France and Italy. Six and one-half of Fogg's 80 days were used up. He was exactly on schedule.

A Stamp for a Passport

Never bothering to see the remarkable sights of Suez, Fogg closed his date book and sat down to breakfast. He was always much more concerned about time than place.

Diary of a Trip

Off the Ship in Suez

Chapter 8
Passepartout Talks Too Much to Fix

Detective Fix joined Passepartout outside the consulate and began a conversation.

"Well, how do you like Suez?"

"We are traveling so fast that I can hardly remember where we are."

"This is Suez, a city in Egypt."

"That means we are on the continent of Africa!" said Passepartout. "I never thought that my master and I would travel further than Paris. I would have loved to stay in Paris, but we just whizzed through."

"You must be in a great hurry."

"I'm not, but my master is. We didn't even pack suitcases—only a carpet bag. I have to buy some clothes here."

Fix was surprised and excited by these remarks. He assured the servant that there was plenty of time to go to a men's store.

"It's only 12:00," said Passepartout, "it is only eight minutes before 10:00."

"Your watch is slow," said Fix.

"That's impossible!"

"Then it must be set for London time, which is two hours behind that of Suez. You should reset your watch when you travel to other countries."

"Reset my watch? Never!"

"It won't agree with the sun if you don't reset it."

"Too bad for the sun," declared the servant, putting the watch in his pocket.

"Did you leave London in a hurry?" asked Fix.

Passepartout Refuses to Reset His Watch.

"You bet we did! Last Friday night at 8:00, my master came home from his club, and less than an hour later we were gone."

"But where is your master going?"

"Around the world in 80 days! He says he made a bet that he could do it, but that's too crazy to believe. Something else must be afoot."

"Ah! So Mr. Fogg is a strange man?"

"Very strange."

"Is he rich?"

"He must be. He's carrying loads of brand new banknotes with him, and he offered the captain of the *Mongolia* a reward if he gets us to India ahead of schedule. By the way, is Bombay far from here?"

"Yes," answered Fix, "it's a ten-day trip by sea."

"Oh dear," sighed Passepartout, "my gas burner will be on for a long time. My gas bill will be higher than the wages my master pays me."

A Secret Too Crazy to Believe!

Fix wasn't listening any more. He dashed to the consul's office.

"I've found the robber for sure," he shouted. "He pretends to be traveling around the world on a bet with some friends. He bet that he could make the journey in 80 days."

"He's a smart fellow, indeed," said the consul. "He'll throw the police off his track and then return to London."

Fix decided to follow Fogg to Bombay. He sent a telegraph to London asking the police to send the arrest warrant to India. Then he boarded the steamer *Mongolia* for the Suez-to-Bombay run.

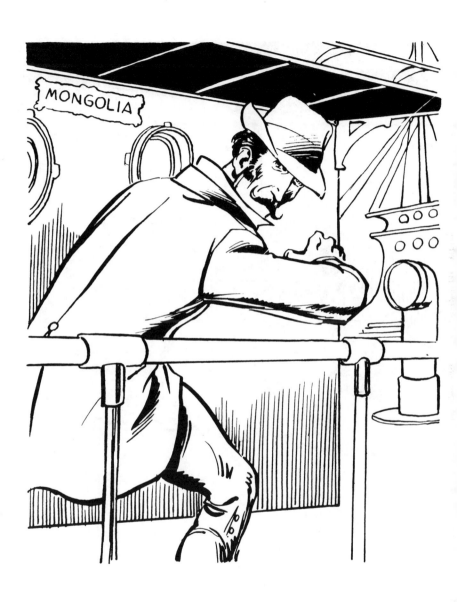

Fix Boards the Steamer, *Mongolia*.

A Conversation on Deck

Chapter 9
On the Way to India

The steamer made good time across the Red Sea and the Indian Ocean. Phileas Fogg occupied himself with four hearty meals each day and, of course, with whist. Passepartout went up on deck and met Detective Fix.

"What a pleasant surprise to see you again!" said the servant. "Where are you traveling to?"

"To Bombay. I work for an English company there," answered Fix, taking care not to reveal the real nature of his mission.

"Well, I hope to see the sights in India,"

said Passepartout. "To spend one's time running from one train or boat to another is stupid—not to mention talk of going around the world in 80 days!"

"Maybe your master is going to perform some secret mission during this trip," said Fix, hoping to get some more information about Fogg's plans.

"If so, I know nothing about it," Passepartout replied.

The *Mongolia* stopped at Aden, in Arabia, to take on coal, and on October 20—two days ahead of schedule—it sailed into Bombay. Phileas Fogg gave the captain a handsome reward for giving him those two extra days. They were sure to be needed to make up for time lost later in the journey.

A Stop in Aden, Arabia

Dinner in Bombay

Chapter 10
Passepartout Leaves His Shoes Behind

Phileas Fogg and Passepartout got off the steamer at 4:00. In four hours the train would leave Bombay, on the west coast of India, for Calcutta, in the northeast.

Caring nothing for the sights of India, Fogg went directly to the consulate for a visa and then to the railroad station for dinner. Detective Fix went to the police station, but the arrest warrant for the bank robber had not arrived.

Passepartout bought shirts and socks for his master. Then he wandered into a beautiful Indian temple, or pagoda. He didn't know that visitors were supposed to leave their shoes at the entrances of pagodas. No sooner had he entered the building than three Indian priests knocked him down, tore off his shoes, and beat him with their fists. Passepartout leaped to his feet, knocked over two of his attackers, and fled to escape the third.

At five minutes before 8:00, the servant, shoeless, dashed into the railroad station and told Phileas Fogg what had happened. Fix, hiding nearby, overheard the conversation.

"Ah!" thought the detective. "Passepartout has committed a crime in India. That should make it easier for me to arrest his master. Fogg must be held responsible for his servant's actions."

Indian Priests Attack Passepartout.

Sir Francis Cromarty Knows India Well.

Chapter 11
A Long Ride on an Elephant

As the train left the station, Phileas Fogg noticed that Sir Francis Cromarty, one of his whist partners from the steamer *Mongolia*, was aboard. Sir Francis, an English army officer, spent most of his time in India and knew the country as well as any Indian. Fogg, however, wasn't interested in learning more about India. He was too busy figuring out how many days and hours of his round-the-world trip had gone by.

"See those mountains?" said Sir Francis. "A few years ago, we would have met such a long delay here that you would have lost your bet. The railroad used to stop here, and the passengers would have to cross the mountains on horses."

"That wouldn't have ruined my travel plans at all," snapped Phileas Fogg. "I knew there would be certain problems."

"Indeed, you may still run into trouble over your servant's behavior at the pagoda. The government protects Indian religions and customs very strictly."

At 8:00 the train stopped, and the conductor ordered all the passengers to get off. They were in the middle of a forest!

"Where are we?" asked Phileas Fogg.

"At the village of Kholby," replied the conductor. "The railroad isn't finished. There is no track between here and Allahabad, a distance of 50 miles."

"But the newspapers said the railroad runs all through India now," Fogg protested.

The Track Ends.

"The papers made a mistake."

"Why, then, do you sell tickets from Bombay to Calcutta?"

"With the understanding that passengers will find their own way of getting from Kholby to Allahabad."

"This is a terrible delay for you, Mr. Fogg," said Sir Francis.

"It's okay. I'm two days ahead of schedule. Today is October 22. A steamer leaves Calcutta for Hong Kong on October 25. We will reach Calcutta by then."

Fogg saw a man with an elephant and decided to buy it at any cost for the trip to Calcutta. The owner didn't want to sell the animal but finally accepted 2,000 pounds. Fogg then hired a young man from the Parsee caste, or class, of India to serve as an elephant driver and guide.

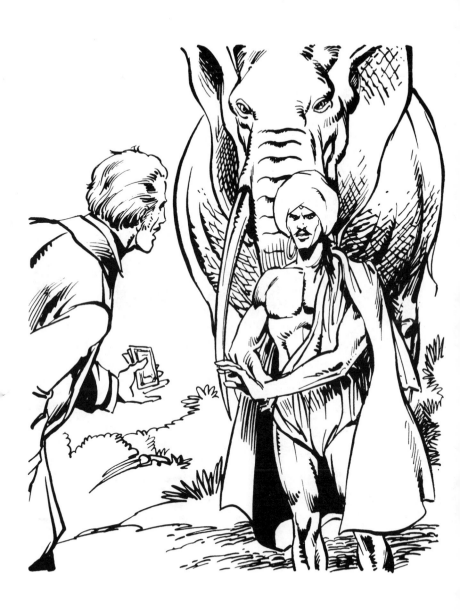

Fogg Buys an Elephant.

A Procession of Hindu Priests

Chapter 12
An Adventure in the Indian Forest

Phileas Fogg and Sir Francis sat on the elephant's neck; Passepartout sat on his back. They passed through an area peopled by fierce tribes with savage customs. Suddenly, the elephant stopped. Loud voices came through the trees.

"A procession of Brahmins is heading this way," said the Parsee. "Let's hide!" Brahmins are the priests of the Indian religion of Hinduism.

Soon the priests came into view, followed by a large crowd of people chanting. Carried along on a platform was a statue of the Hindu goddess Kali, with four arms and a red body. The Brahmins also dragged along a young woman dressed in a beautiful robe and jewelry. She had very light skin and looked more like a European than an Indian. Behind her came men holding sabers and guns, and carrying the body of an old man dressed like a Hindu prince. The Parsee explained that the body was that of the young woman's husband, who was an Indian rajah, or prince.

"The woman will be taken to a pagoda to spend the night," said the Parsee. "Tomorrow at dawn, she will be burned alive as a human sacrifice to the gods!"

"I have 12 hours to spare," cried out Phileas Fogg. "Let us stop and save this woman!"

A Human Sacrifice to the Gods!

A Forced Marriage!

Chapter 13
Aouda

Aouda, as the young woman was called, was also a Parsee. Famed for her beauty, she was the daughter of a rich merchant in Bombay and had received an English education. After her father died, she was forced to marry the old rajah. When she ran away, she was caught and brought back. Now she faced a horrible death.

The would-be rescuers hid in the trees near the pagoda to await nightfall. They hoped to slip past the Brahmins into the pagoda, but guards with torches and sabers stood at all the entrances. Passepartout, noticing that the Brahmins were drunk, began to work on another plan of rescue.

Dawn came, and the hour of sacrifice was at hand. The Brahmins built a platform, or funeral pyre, and laid the rajah's body on it. Then the priests led Aouda out of the pagoda. She had been drugged and was helpless to free herself. She was stretched out beside her husband's body. The priests soaked the funeral pyre with oil and set a torch to it. Flames leaped up at once.

Suddenly, cries of terror came from the crowd. The old rajah was alive! He stood up, took his wife in his arms, and, surrounded by fire and smoke, climbed down from the funeral pyre. He walked over took Phileas Fogg and said, "Let us be off!"

Passepartout was the "rajah." In the moments before dawn, under cover of darkness, he had hidden the body of the real rajah and placed himself on the funeral pyre instead.

Passepartout Rescues Princess Aouda.

Aouda, still in a drugged sleep, was lifted onto the elephant, and the travelers rode quickly through the forest. When the Brahmins discovered the trick, they ran after the elephant, shooting bullets and arrows. It was too late, however. Aouda was a safe distance away.

Escape from the Brahmins

Awakening from the Drugs

Chapter 14
Phileas Fogg Gains a New Travel Companion

Passepartout was delighted at the success of his rescue mission. Sir Francis, however, warned that if Aouda didn't leave India she would be recaptured sooner or later and sacrificed.

At 10:00, the travelers arrived at the Allahabad railroad station. Aouda awoke slowly from the effects of the drugs. She was indeed beautiful and spoke English very well.

Phileas Fogg said good-bye to the Parsee, giving him not only the money promised for his services, but the elephant as well. Fogg, Passepartout, Aouda and Sir Francis then boarded the train for Calcutta.

Aouda awoke to find herself dressed in European-style clothes and traveling on a train with perfect strangers! Fogg offered to take her out of India so that the Brahmins could not recapture her. He invited her to go with him to the colony of Hong Kong, which lay off the coast of China and was ruled by England. Aouda said that she would look up her cousin, Jeejeeh, who lived in Hong Kong.

Sir Francis got off the train in Benares. The next morning it arrived at Calcutta. Phileas Fogg had gained two days between London and Bombay and lost two days traveling across India, so he was exactly on schedule.

Fogg Takes Aouda Out of India.

Arrested in Calcutta

Chapter 15
A Day in Court

"Are you Mr. Phileas Fogg?" asked a policeman at the Calcutta station.

"Yes."

"And is this man your servant?"

"He is."

"Please follow me."

Fogg, Passepartout and Aouda were taken to a room with bars on the windows.

"You must appear before the judge at 8:30," said the policeman.

"We are prisoners!" shouted Passepartout. "Now we shall miss the Hong Kong steamer."

"Leave me here and go," said Aouda. "If you hadn't rescued me, you would not be in this prison."

"Don't be silly," snapped Phileas Fogg. "Besides, we'll all be on the steamer by noon."

At 8:30, the policeman led the prisoners to a courtroom. Three priests stood in front of the judge. They charged Fogg and Passepartout with misbehaving in a Brahmin holy place.

"I admit our guilt," Fogg said, "but the priests were about to perform a human sacrifice!"

"That's right," added Passepartout. "These priests are from the pagoda of Pillaji."

"No," said the priests. "We are from Bombay. Here is a pair of shoes that was left behind."

"Those are mine!" cried Passepartout.

Detective Fix had promised the priests a reward if they would follow Passepartout to

"We'll All Be on the Steamer by Noon."

Calcutta. Now Fix was hiding in the court-room. His plan was to delay Phileas Fogg so that he could not leave India before the arrest warrant arrived for the bank robber.

"Since you have admitted your guilt," the judge told Passepartout, "and since English law protects Indian religions very strictly, I order you to spend 15 days in jail and pay a fine of 300 pounds."

The judge then turned to Phileas Fogg.

"A master must be responsible for the acts of his hired servant. Therefore, Mr. Fogg, I order you to spend a week in jail and pay a 150-pound fine."

Fix rubbed his hands in glee. Surely a week would be enough time for the arrest warrant to come from London.

"I offer bail," declared Phileas Fogg.

"All right," said the judge, "but the bail will be 1,000 pounds for each man. And if you leave India before your sentence is up, the money will not be returned."

15 Days in Jail and a 300-Pound Fine

Fix was furious! The robber was about to escape again! He knew Fogg would gladly leave the bail money behind rather than miss the Hong Kong steamer.

Fogg, Passepartout and Aouda reached the harbor at 11:00 with an hour to spare. Fix decided to follow them to Hong Kong.

Hurrying to Catch the Hong Kong Steamer

Exchanging Life Stories

Chapter 16
Detective Fix's Predicament

Phileas Fogg sailed from India to Hong Kong on the steamer *Rangoon*. During the trip, which normally took 10 to 12 days, Aouda related the story of her life, and Passepartout told her about his master's 20,000-pound bet. Fogg himself spent long hours with Aouda but rarely spoke to her. He seemed unmoved by her great beauty. Phileas Fogg was a strange man indeed!

Fix spent much of the trip hidden in his cabin. He had asked the London police to send the arrest warrant for the bank robber on to

Hong Kong. That was the last English-ruled place Fogg would visit before traveling to China, Japan and America. Once he left English soil, the robber might escape for good.

Did Fix dare tell Passepartout who he really was? He felt sure that the servant had not taken part in the bank robbery and didn't even know that Fogg was a thief. If Fix could persuade Passepartout that he might have to share responsibility for his master's crime, perhaps he could get his cooperation in arresting Fogg. On the other hand, Passepartout might reveal Fix's real indentity.

Fix approached the servant on deck and, with an air of pretended surprise, asked what he was doing on the *Rangoon.*

"I should ask you the same question," said Passepartout. "I thought we had left you at Bombay. Are you going around the world too?"

A Surprise Meeting

"No," replied the detective. "I will stay at Hong Kong for awhile. Tell me, how is Mr. Fogg?"

"He's quite well and still on schedule. Did you know that we also have a young lady traveling with us?"

Fix tried again to look surprised. Passepartout told him about their adventures in India, including the rescue of Aouda and the affair with the shoes in the pagoda at Bombay. He didn't know, of course, that Fix had plotted to get him in trouble with the Bombay priests.

"Are you taking the young lady to Europe?" the detective asked.

"No. We will leave her with a cousin in Hong Kong."

Fix saved his other questions for later, for fear of making Passepartout suspicious.

Fix Has Many Questions.

Passepartout Becomes Suspicious.

Chapter 17
A Trip from Singapore to Hong Kong

Passepartout wondered why Fix kept following them around the world, but not in his wildest dreams could he have imagined the real reason. He finally decided that Fix must be a spy sent by the members of the Reform Club to make sure that Phileas Fogg was really going around the world.

"Gentlemen of the Reform Club," Passepartout said to himself, "you'll be sorry for treating my master like this!" The servant said nothing to Mr. Fogg, however, for fear of insulting him.

On October 31, the *Rangoon* sailed into

Singapore to take on coal. Phileas Fogg noted in his diary that the ship was a half day ahead of schedule. Hong Kong was still 1,300 miles away. If he could reach Hong Kong in six days, he would be able to catch the steamer for Yokohama, Japan, on November 6.

After Phileas Fogg had left the ship with Aouda for a carriage ride through Singapore, Fix cornered Passepartout once again.

"You seem to be in a great hurry to reach Hong Kong," he said.

"A very great hurry," answered Passepartout.

"Mr. Fogg, I suppose, wants to catch the steamer for Yokohama."

"That's right."

"Do you really believe, then, that he intends to go around the world?"

"Of course I do. Don't you?"

"No, I don't believe a word of it."

"You're very sly," said Passepartout. "Al-

A Carriage Ride Through Singapore

ways full of tricks! Tell me, will we be so unlucky to lose you when we get to Hong Kong?"

"I'm not sure. . . ." Fix answered.

"Ah, but you should come with us. You already have followed us from Suez to India and now to China. Japan will be next, and then America!"

Fix was getting more and more nervous.

"Do you make much money at your job?" asked Passepartout.

"That depends," Fix said. "Sometimes my luck is good, sometimes bad. However, I don't pay my own travel expenses."

"I'm sure of that," the servant retorted, thinking that the Reform Club members had hired Fix as a spy.

This conversation ended when Phileas Fogg and Aouda returned to the ship. But Fix was worried. Did Passepartout guess who he really was? And, if so, had he told Phileas Fogg?

Fogg and Aouda Return to the Ship.

A Storm Delays the *Rangoon*.

Chapter 18
Arrival at Hong Kong

On November 3, a terrible storm hit the *Rangoon*. Calm seas returned the next day, but it was too late. The steamer, due in Hong Kong on November 5, didn't arrive until November 6.

"When does the next ship leave for Yokohama?" Fogg asked the captain.

"The *Carnatic* leaves tomorrow at high tide. It was supposed to sail yesterday, but one of its boilers had to be fixed."

This was indeed a stroke of luck for Phileas Fogg! If the *Carnatic*'s boiler had not broken down, she would have sailed, and Fogg would have to wait a week for the next steamer. As things stood, Mr. Fogg was 24 hours behind schedule, but the time probably could be made up later.

With 16 hours to spend in Hong Kong, Fogg left Passepartout with Aouda and set out to search for the young woman's cousin, Jee-jeeh. He learned, however, that the cousin had moved from Hong Kong to Europe. There was thus no choice but to take Aouda along on the rest of the journey around the world. The young woman was, in fact, delighted by this turn of events. She had fallen in love with Phileas Fogg.

Searching Hong Kong for Aouda's Cousin

Buying Tickets on the *Carnatic*

Chapter 19
Detective Fix Gets Passepartout into a "Fix"

"Have you decided to travel with us to America, Mr. Fix?" asked Passepartout.

"Yes," replied the detective, who in fact was determined to keep Phileas Fogg from leaving Hong Kong before the arrest warrant arrived.

"Good! I didn't think you could bear to be apart from us," said the servant, chuckling. "Let's get cabins on the *Carnatic*."

A man at the ticket office announced that the boiler was fixed and the *Carnatic* would sail that evening. Passepartout wanted to tell Phileas Fogg the good news at once, but Fix invited him to a tavern.

The customers at the tavern were either drinking liquor or smoking opium, a very powerful sleep-producing drug. Smokers overcome by the opium were carried to a large bed at one end of the tavern. Passepartout shared a bottle of wine with Fix and then rose to return to Phileas Fogg.

"Wait!" cried Fix. "I must tell you something very important before you leave."

"Tell me tomorrow!" snapped Passepartout. "There is no time now!"

"What I have to say concerns Mr. Fogg."

Passepartout sat down again.

"You have guessed who I am?" began Fix.

"Of course."

"Then I'll tell you everything."

"I already know everything. But let me tell you that those gentlemen have gone to a lot of trouble and expense for nothing!"

An Opium Tavern in Hong Kong

"For nothing?" exclaimed Fix. "A very large sum of money is involved!"

"Yes, 20,000 pounds."

"It's 55,000 pounds," Fix corrected.

"What?" shouted Passepartout. "Has Mr. Fogg really dared to bet 55,000 pounds? If so, that is all the more reason to hurry and tell him the change in the *Carnatic*'s timetable."

"Wait!" cried Fix. "Help me! If I succeed, I will get 2,000 pounds as a reward. I'll give you 500 pounds!"

"Help you?"

"Yes. I must keep Phileas Fogg in Hong Kong for a few days."

"Do you know what you're asking, Mr. Fix? It's not enough for you to follow my master and question his honesty. These gentlemen you work for also want to stop him from making his trip around the world. What a shameless plot! And you think of yourselves as gentlemen! You go back and tell the members

110

"What a Shameless Plot!"

of the Reform Club that Phileas Fogg is an honest man, and he wins his bets fairly!"

"Who *do* you think I am?" asked Fix, who was really puzzled by these remarks.

"Listen, Mr. Fix. I discovered that you were hired by the members of the Reform Club to try and stop Phileas Fogg from completing his journey around the world. However, I didn't tell my master because I didn't want to hurt him."

"Mr. Passepartout, I am not in fact a spy for the Reform Club. I am a police detective. Here is my badge to prove it!"

"But what do you want from me?"

"I will tell you. Mr. Fogg's bet that he could travel around the world in 80 days was just a trick to keep you and the Reform Club members from discovering why he really had to leave London in a hurry."

"What was that?"

"On September 28, a man robbed the Bank

"I Am a Police Detective."

of England of 55,000 pounds. Someone saw him and described him to the police. The robber can be none other than Phileas Fogg."

"Nonsense!" snapped Passepartout. "My master is an honest man!"

"How can you be sure?" Fix prodded. "The very day you came to work for him, he made a wager and left the country without even taking time to pack suitcases. He also took along a large role of banknotes."

Passepartout reflected on Fix's words. Indeed, he hardly knew Phileas Fogg when the trip began. Nevertheless, he had seen Mr. Fogg's generosity in helping the beggar at the London railroad station, giving the valuable elephant to the Parsee, and, above all, risking his fortune (and his life) to stop and rescue Aouda.

"Listen!" said Fix. "I must delay Phileas Fogg in Hong Kong until the arrest warrant arrives. If you help me do this, I will share

Fix Talks About the Bank Robbery.

with you my 2,000-pound reward for catching the robber."

"Never!" screamed Passepartout, who was quite drunk by now. "Besides, my master is not a robber!"

"Then you refuse to help me?"

"Yes, I refuse."

"Very well. Let's forget the whole thing and drink some more," said Fix.

The liquor made Passepartout sleepy. As he leaned weakly against his chair, Fix slipped an opium pipe between his lips. The servant sank into a drugged sleep.

"Good!" Fix chuckled to himself. "Now Mr. Fogg will not learn that the *Carnatic* is sailing tonight!"

Fix Drugs Passepartout with Opium.

"I'd Like to See Your Servant."

Chapter 20
Fix Comes Face to Face with Fogg

Phileas Fogg and Aouda shopped and dined in Hong Kong. When Passepartout failed to appear at bedtime, Fogg decided he must be enjoying himself before sailing the following morning. Fogg and Aouda reached the harbor to find that the *Carnatic* had left the night before. There was still no sign of Passepartout.

"I'd like to see your servant. Is he with you?" asked a man on the dock. It was Detective Fix. He pretended surprise at the news of Passepartout's absence.

"Maybe he boarded the *Carnatic* without us," suggested Phileas Fogg.

"Oh, did you plan to sail on the *Carnatic*? So did I. Now we will have to wait a week for another steamer for Yokohama."

"There must be other boats ready to sail," said Fogg. "We'll find one." Just then a sailor approached.

"I have a vessel for you, sir."

"Does she travel fast?" asked Fogg.

"Of course. Where do you wish to go?"

"To Yokohama."

"You must be joking! I can't possibly take you that far!"

"I missed the *Carnatic*," Fogg explained. "I must reach Yokohama by November 14 in order to catch a boat for America. I can offer you 100 pounds per day, plus 200 pounds more as a reward for getting me there on time."

"I'm truly sorry, sir," said the captain. "It's

Looking for a Boat

too risky to make such a long trip in my little boat, especially at this time of year. Anyway, Yokohama is more than 1,600 miles from Hong Kong. We'd never make it on time. Maybe something else could be arranged, however."

"What's that?" asked Fogg eagerly.

"We could sail to Shanghai, which is only 800 miles from here. The American steamer starts at Shanghai and makes a stop at Yokohama. The steamer leaves Shanghai on November 11 at 7:00 in the morning. That gives us four days to reach Shanghai."

"It's a deal! My name is Phileas Fogg."

"I am John Bunsby, captain of the Tankadere."

"Would you like to join us, Mr. Fix?" Fogg asked the detective.

"Yes, and thank you very much!"

Captain Bunsby and the *Tankadere*

Covering the Miles to Shanghai

Chapter 21
A Dangerous Voyage on the *Tankadere*

Fix was embarrassed to be traveling at Phileas Fogg's expense, but he also felt that the "robber" owed him something for putting him to so much trouble.

"What a clever man Fogg is!" thought Fix. "He'll go all the way to America to throw the police off his track and then settle down to enjoy his stolen money!"

By sunrise on November 8, the *Tankadere* had traveled more than 100 miles; by evening, she had gone 220 miles. Captain Bunsby, eager for his reward, spared no effort to reach

Shanghai on time. The following day, however, a terrible storm hit the ship.

"It's a typhoon!" shouted the captain. "We must sail for the nearest port!!"

"There is only one port for us," said Phileas Fogg, "and that is Shanghai!" It was useless to argue against such a man.

At 7:00, the hour that the Yokohama steamer was due to depart from Shanghai, Phileas Fogg was three miles from Shanghai harbor. Suddenly the steamer appeared on the waves.

"Signal her!" Fogg ordered Captain Bunsby. "Hoist your flag!"

Bunsby ran the flag up at half mast—a signal that his ship was in danger. He also fired the small cannon that he kept on the deck for use in fog.

Would the steamer respond?

Signaling the Steamer

A Drugged Sleep on the *Carnatic*

Chapter 22
Passepartout Arrives Alone in Japan

On November 7 at 6:30 P.M., the *Carnatic* set sail from Hong Kong. Passepartout was on board. He had been carried by two waiters to the bed in the tavern. Struggling against the effects of the opium, he dreamed of his duty to tell Phileas Fogg about the *Carnatic*'s new timetable. Somehow he dragged himself to the harbor and jumped upon the *Carnatic* just as it was ready to depart. Then he fell into a drugged sleep on the deck.

When Passepartout awoke, the ship was already 150 miles from Hong Kong. The servant recalled with horror the events in the tavern.

"At least I didn't miss the steamer," he said to himself. "But I must find Mr. Fogg right away and explain everything!" Fogg and Aouda were nowhere to be found.

"Can you tell me what cabin Mr. Phileas Fogg is in?" he asked a crew member.

"We have no young lady on board. Here is the passenger list. Look for yourself!"

Suddenly Passepartout realized that he hadn't told Fogg when the ship was leaving. Mr. Fogg would surely lose his bet and might even be in jail in Hong Kong!

Phileas Fogg Is Not on the Passenger List.

Passepartout Dresses Like a Beggar.

Chapter 23
Clowns with Long Noses

On November 13, the *Carnatic* arrived in Yokohama. Passepartout was alone in a strange land and had no money at all. By the next day, he was so hungry that he was ready to beg for food, but he was too well dressed to be a beggar. He met a man selling old clothes and exchanged his European outfit for a Japanese-style coat, a faded hat and a few pieces of silver. He spent the money at once for breakfast.

A clown carrying a large sign printed in English attracted Passepartout's attention.

The sign announced that the circus would give one last performance that day before sailing to America. Passepartout followed the clown and came to the tent of the circus manager.

"Would you like a servant, sir?"

"No, I have two servants already."

"Can't I be of use to you in any way?"

"None at all."

"That's too bad, for I would really like to go to America with you."

"Ah," said the manager, "you are not Japanese! Why are you dressed like that?"

"I am, in fact, a Frenchman."

"Can you make funny faces?"

"Of course."

"A French clown would be very popular in America. Are you quite strong?"

"Yes," answered Passepartout, "especially after I eat a good meal."

"Can you sing?"

A Job with the Circus?

"Yes."

"If you can sing while standing on your head, with a top spinning on your left foot and a saber balanced on your right foot, then you're hired!"

Passepartout joined a group of clowns called the Long Noses. They wore costumes with wings and had very long noses made of bamboo wood. They performed tricks by dancing and leaping on each others' noses. The last and most exciting act of the circus was to be a pyramid, or tower, of clowns.

Passepartout and some of the other clowns had to form the base, or bottom, of the pyramid. They stood side by side with their long noses pointed straight out. Another row of clowns stood on top of their noses, then another and another. Each layer of the pyramid was narrower than the layer below. Finally, the clown at the very top of the pyramid took his place, balanced on the noses of the two

The Pyramid of Clowns

clowns underneath him. The audience was thrilled.

Suddenly the whole pyramid collapsed!

It was Passepartout's fault. He had lost his balance and brought the clowns above him tumbling down. Passepartout ran off the stage. Throwing himself at the feet of a man in the audience, he cried out. "My master, you're here!"

"Is that you?" exclaimed Phileas Fogg. "Let us hurry and catch the steamer!"

Fogg, Aouda and Passepartout left the circus tent quickly. Mr. Fogg paid the manager for the damage to his act caused by Passepartout. The party boarded the steamer at 6:30, just as it was about to depart. Passepartout still wore his long nose and his clown costume, complete with wings.

The Pyramid Collapses.

The *Tankadere* Reaches Shanghai.

Chapter 24
Phileas Fogg Crosses the Pacific Ocean

Although Phileas Fogg and Aouda had missed the *Carnatic*, they reached Japan only one day after Passepartout. As their small boat, the *Tankadere*, sailed into Shanghai, Captain John Bunsby signaled the steamer, which was just setting out for Japan. When he saw the *Tankadere*'s flag flying at half-mast and heard the boom of the little cannon, the steamer's captain thought the little boat was in trouble and sailed over to help. Phileas Fogg paid John Bunsby his reward—plus an extra 550 pounds—and boarded the steamer

141

with Aouda. They reached Japan on the morning of November 14.

Fogg learned that Passepartout had arrived on the *Carnatic* the day before. He hoped to find his servant before the American steamer departed that very night, but Yokohama was so big that the search seemed useless.

Pure chance brought Fogg to the circus. He never would have recognized Passepartout in his clown costume standing with the others on the stage. The servant, however, saw Fogg and was so startled that he shifted his position to get a better look. This sudden movement made the whole pyramid fall down.

Passepartout decided not to tell his master yet about his conversation with Detective Fix in the tavern in Hong Kong. He simply explained that he had not shown up because he had drunk too much liquor and smoked too

Boarding the Steamer to Japan

much opium. Phileas Fogg forgave him and handed him some money to buy real clothes. Within an hour, the clown costume and the long nose were nothing but a bad memory.

Phileas Fogg and his party sailed from Yokohama to San Francisco, California, on the steamer *General Grant*. By traveling at 12 miles an hour, she could cross the Pacific Ocean in 21 days, thus arriving on December 2. This schedule would give Phileas Fogg time to reach New York by December 11 and London by December 20. He was not due back at the Reform Club until December 21.

Aouda worried that something still might upset the timetable. Passepartout, however, explained that the strange countries of China and Japan were behind them and that nothing could go wrong in an advanced country like America.

Aouda was beginning to fall in love with Phileas Fogg. Besides being thankful to him

The Long Nose Is a Bad Memory.

for saving her life, she found him worthy and generous. Fogg, however, remained cold and silent, and no one, including Aouda, could guess his inner thoughts.

Nine days after leaving Yokohama, Phileas Fogg had traveled across exactly one-half of the earth. November 23 found the *General Grant* 180 degrees across the globe from London. Fogg had used up more than half of the 80 days, however, because it wasn't possible to make the whole journey in a straight line around the globe. Such a trip would have been about 12,000 miles. In fact, Fogg had already used up 52 days and traveled 17,500 miles in a journey totaling about 26,000 miles. Thus, he had completed more than two thirds of his trip and had 28 days left.

Best of all, Fix was no longer around to cause trouble—or so Mr. Fogg thought.

On November 23, Passepartout noticed

Fogg's Inner Thoughts

that his watch, which he had refused to reset according to Fix's advice, showed the exact same time as the ship's clock. Passepartout didn't know it, but, in fact, there was a 12-hour time difference; he was exactly halfway across the world from London. The servant's watch now said 9:00 in the evening, but in London it was 9:00 in the morning!

Detective Fix was at that moment aboard the *General Grant*! He had gone to the English consul in Yokohama and finally received the arrest warrant for Phileas Fogg. The warrant had actually been sent aboard the steamer *Carnatic*. However, since Fogg had already left English territory, the warrant would be no good until he returned to England! Therefore, the detective had no choice but to follow the "robber" the rest of the way around the world.

"It seems like the rascal really does plan to go around the world to throw the police off

Checking the Time Again

his track," Fix said to himself. "The problem is that Fogg has spent so much money already that there might not be anything left for my reward when I arrest him."

Fix recognized Passepartout, even though he wore a clown costume, when he and Aouda boarded the *General Grant*. The detective wanted to hide, but that very day he ran into the servant on deck. Passepartout grabbed him by the throat and knocked him sprawling on the floor.

"Are you finished?" asked Fix.

"For now, yes."

"Then let me have a word with you."

"But . . ."

"In your master's interests."

Passepartout reluctantly followed Fix.

"You knocked me down with your fists, and I deserved it," said the detective. "Now, listen to me! Up to now, I have been Phileas Fogg's enemy, but now I'm ready to help him."

"So you believe that he's an honest man

A Knockout Blow!

like I said?"

"No, I think he's a rascal," answered Fix. "But you won't find out until we return to England whether you're working for a thief or a true gentleman. Up to now I tried to keep Mr. Fogg on English soil in order to arrest him. That's why I sent the Bombay priests after you, got you drunk in Hong Kong, separated you from your master, and made Fogg miss the Yokohama steamer."

Passepartout listened quietly but kept his fists clenched.

"Now Fogg seems to be returning to England," continued Fix. "I want to see him get there as quickly as possible. This is in your interest too."

"Very well," answered Passepartout, "but I'll break your neck if you do anything else to delay or hurt my master."

On December 3, the *General Grant* sailed into San Francisco harbor. Phileas Fogg had reached America exactly on schedule!

San Francisco Harbor

In San Francisco for a Visa

Chapter 25
A Short Stay in San Francisco

A train was due to leave San Francisco for New York at 6:00 in the evening. Fogg and Aouda ate lunch and then went to the consulate for a visa. On the way there, they met Detective Fix.

"I didn't know that we all crossed the Pacific on the *General Grant*," Fix lied. "By the way, I have to return to England on business. I hope to have the pleasure of your company for the rest of the trip."

"My pleasure," answered Phileas Fogg, who still didn't have the faintest idea that

Fix was a detective. The three of them walked toward Montgomery Street, where a huge crowd had gathered.

"Hurrah for Camerfield!" cried some voices.

"Hurrah for Mandiboy!" cried others.

It was a political rally.

"We should leave," warned Fix. "Englishmen should stay out of American politics."

It was too late for Phileas Fogg to escape. He and Fix were surrounded on one side by the voters favoring Camerfield and on the other by those favoring Mandiboy. While Fogg was trying to protect Aouda, a tall, broad-shouldered man with a red beard and a flushed face raised his clenched fist. Fogg would have received a terrible blow had not Fix stepped in between him and his attacker. The blow crushed the detective's silk hat and knocked him to the ground.

"Yankee!" shouted Phileas Fogg to the American.

A Political Rally

"Englishman!" screamed the ruffian. "We shall meet again. What's your name?"

"Phileas Fogg. What's yours?"

"Colonel Stamp Proctor."

Having finally escaped the crowds, Fogg and Fix went to a tailor to have their rumpled clothes ironed. Then they met Passepartout for dinner. Aouda told him about their adventure, and he noted to himself that Fix had indeed behaved like a friend rather than a troublemaker.

After dinner, Phileas Fogg and his party hired a carriage to take them to the railroad station. The train for New York was boarding.

"I must come back to America someday to even the score with Colonel Proctor," said Fogg. "An Englishman has to defend his honor."

Fogg later asked the conductor why the crowd on Montgomery Street had been so noisy and angry.

Repairing the Damaged Clothes

"It was a political meeting, sir. There is going to be an election."

"It must be an election for an army general," said Fogg.

"Oh, no, sir! It is for a justice of the peace!"

The Conductor Explains the Election.

A Herd of Buffalo Blocks the Tracks.

Chapter 26
An Encounter with Buffalo

There are 3,768 miles separating San Francisco from New York. In 1872, the year of Phileas Fogg's trip, it took a train seven days to cover that distance. If Fogg could reach New York by December 11, he could catch the Atlantic Ocean steamer for Liverpool, England.

The first delay on the railroad came when a herd of buffalo began to cross the tracks. The herd numbered in the thousands, and the buffalo moved very slowly. Phileas Fogg, as always, took the delay in stride. Passepartout was furious, however. He wanted to shoot the animals, but he knew that such action would only kill a small number of them and that their bodies would block the track further.

There was nothing to do but wait.

"What a country!" shouted Passepartout. "Animals should not be allowed to stop trains! Why not just run the buffalo down?"

In fact, the force of the engine against the buffalo could easily derail the train, thus causing an even worse delay.

It took three hours for all the buffalo to cross the tracks. The train could not move on until nightfall. At 8:00, it arrived at Salt Lake City in the state of Utah.

Arriving in Salt Lake City

Elder Hitch Gives a Lecture.

Chapter 27
Passepartout Learns Some Mormon History

Salt Lake City was a center of the Mormon religion. Mormon leaders often gave lectures aboard railroad trains to seek new followers. Passepartout, who had heard that Mormons were permitted to have more than one wife, decided to attend a lecture by a certain Elder Hitch.

Most of the audience quickly lost interest in the lecture, and soon Passepartout found himself alone in the car with the Mormon. Elder Hitch shouted, "We Mormons will never bow to force and pressure! We have been driven out of many parts of the United States, but we will continue to practice our religion! Will you join us, brother?"

"No!" snapped Passepartout, walking swiftly back to Phileas Fogg's car. By this time, the train's whistle was announcing that they were ready to leave the Mormon town and continue their journey east.

As the train was about to pull out of the Salt Lake City station, a man ran breathlessly onto the platform. He dashed along the track and jumped aboard the moving train. When he recovered his breath, he declared that he had run away after a quarrel with his wife.

"But how many other wives do you have?" asksed Passepartout.

"I have only one wife," the man replied, "and that is quite enough!"

A Stranger Jumps Aboard.

Colonel Stamp Proctor Boards the Train.

Chapter 28
A Jump Across a Bridge

On December 7, the train stopped at the Green River station, and Aouda saw Colonel Stamp Proctor on the platform.

"We must keep this man away from Mr. Fogg!" she whispered to Passepartout and Fix.

"Don't worry," said Fix. "Before he settles with Mr. Fogg, he must settle with me. It was I that he knocked down."

"Mr. Fix," said Aouda, "Mr. Fogg will not let anyone else fight for him. He said that he would return to America just to find the colonel. If they meet now, something terrible might happen!"

"Listen!" said Passepartout. "Let's just make sure that Mr. Fogg doesn't leave his car until we reach New York. That way, he won't see Colonel Proctor. The best way to keep him in his car is to get him into a game of whist!" Luckily, both Aouda and Fix knew how to play whist. Passepartout got two decks of cards.

Suddenly a loud whistle blew, and the train came to a screeching stop. Fogg sent Passepartout to find out what was wrong. The engineer explained that the bridge at Medicine Bow, Wyoming, was not strong enough for the train to cross.

"We have wired Omaha, Nebraska, for a train," the engineer added, "but it won't reach Medicine Bow for at least six hours. It will take us that long to walk to Medicine Bow anyhow."

Keeping Fogg in the Car

"But Medicine Bow is only a mile from here," said Colonel Proctor.

"Yes," replied the engineer, "but it's on the other side of the river!"

"Can't we cross by boat?" asked Passepartout.

"That's impossible. The rains have flooded the river. We'd have to go ten miles to find a ford for crossing."

This would cause a delay. And all of Phileas Fogg's banknotes could do nothing about it! Fogg, however, was too busy playing whist to notice what had happened.

"Gentlemen, there may be a way to cross the bridge after all," said the engineer.

"But the bridge is not safe," said Passepartout.

"It doesn't matter. If we run the train at top speed, we'll have a chance to get across."

Passepartout thought it was too risky.

"At least we might cross the bridge on foot

Fogg Is Too Busy with Whist.

and let the train follow us," he muttered, but no one was listening.

"Don't be afraid!" said Colonel Proctor.

"All aboard!" shouted the conductor.

Phileas Fogg never even lifted his head from the card table.

The engineer backed up the train for almost a mile in order to get a good start. Then the train moved forward again, picking up speed until it reached 100 miles an hour.

Suddenly, like a flash, the train leaped over the bridge! It went five miles further on the other side before the engineer could slow it down. The passengers were safe, but as soon as the train had passed, the bridge fell with a loud crash into the river below.

A Narrow Escape!

"I Would Play a Diamond, Englishman!"

Chapter 29
Duels and Indians

Phileas Fogg's journey from San Francisco to New York was almost half over. The train had gone, 1,382 miles in three days. In another four days it would be in New York. Mr. Fogg was exactly on time.

Fogg and Detective Fix were so busy playing whist that they didn't hear a man coming up behind them.

"I would play a diamond, Englishman!" said Colonel Stamp Proctor.

Phileas Fogg laid the ten of spades on the table.

"I would rather have diamonds played than spades," the colonel insisted, moving toward Fogg as if to grab the card. "You really don't know how to play whist."

Suddenly, Detective Fix stood up.

"You forget, Colonel Proctor, that you must deal with me, for you struck and insulted me in San Francisco."

"No, Mr. Fix," said Phileas Fogg. "This is my affair and I'll handle it. The colonel has insisted that I play a spade. He won't get away with it!"

"I'm ready to fight a duel with you," said Colonel Proctor. "You choose the weapon."

Phileas Fogg went out to the platform, followed by the American.

"Sir, I am in a great hurry to get back to Europe," Fogg explained. "I cannot allow anything to delay me. Will you meet me here in six months?"

"You're just looking for an excuse not to fight. It's now or never!"

Colonel Proctor Is Ready to Duel.

"All right," said Fogg. "Are you going to New York?"

"No. I'm going to Plum Creek," said Proctor. "That's the next station. The train will stop there for ten minutes. That will give us time to exchange a few shots."

"Very well," said Fogg. "I'll stop at Plum Creek." He returned to his car to finish the game of whist.

When the train reached Plum Creek station, the conductor shouted, "Gentlemen, you can't get off! We're 20 minutes late and can't stop here!"

"But we must fight a duel!" cried Fogg.

"How about fighting as we move along?" asked the conductor, and the two men agreed.

The last car of the train was chosen for the duel. Phileas Fogg and Colonel Proctor were to march toward each other from opposite ends of the car and then fire their revolvers.

As the countdown began, gunfire was heard

A Duel at Plum Creek Station

from the front end of the train. A band of Sioux Indians had attacked! They ran through the cars, fighting hand to hand with the screaming passengers. Then they climbed into the engine and tried to stop the train. Instead of closing the steam valve, however, they opened it wide, causing the train to rush forward at top speed.

"Unless the train is stopped in five minutes, we'll all be lost!" shouted the conductor. "Fort Kearney is only two miles away, and the soldiers there can help us!"

"The train will be stopped!" said Passepartout. Before Phileas Fogg could stop him, he opened a door and slipped under the car. A few minutes later, the train came to a stop a few feet from Kearney station.

The Sioux Attack.

Passepartout Stops the Train.

Chapter 30
A Prisoner of the Indians!

By holding onto the metal chains under the cars, Passepartout had managed to swing from the back end of the train to the front. He loosened the safety chain that joined the engine to the other cars, and the jolts of the swiftly moving train broke the engine loose. When the train came to a stop by Fort Kearney, however, Passepartout and two other passengers were missing.

The Indians, who fled at the first sight of the soldiers, had taken the three as prisoners!

"I will find Passepartout, dead or alive!" declared Phileas Fogg to Aouda.

This decision might well cost Fogg his 20,000-pound bet. He could not afford to lose a single day, but he could not abandon his faithful servant.

"Three passengers have been taken prisoner," said Fogg to the commander at Fort Kearney. "Will you go after the Sioux?"

"I can't do that, sir. I must protect the fort from Indian attacks."

"The lives of three men are at stake," Fogg insisted.

"That may be true, but I cannot risk the lives of 50 or 100 men to save three."

"Very well, then, I will go alone!"

"You can't handle the Indians alone!"

"Do you expect me to let Passepartout die after he saved all of our lives?" asked Fogg.

"You are a brave man. I will send 30 men to help you," said the commander. Fogg promised to divide 5,000 dollars among them if they brought the prisoners back alive.

"You Can't Handle the Indians Alone!"

Aouda and Fix waited anxiously for Fogg to return. Fix feared that the "robber" might escape for good with the stolen money.

Suddenly a whistle sounded. The engineer was running the locomotive back to join the stranded train.

"We must start at once," said the conductor. "We're way behind schedule!"

"What about the prisoners?" Aouda asked.

"It is impossible to wait for them!"

"Then I will stay behind," she said.

The train sped off into the distance. Night came, and there was still no sign of Phileas Fogg and the soldiers. At dawn, the fort commander was ready to give up his soldiers as lost. Suddenly they appeared in the distance, along with the prisoners.

The Prisoners Are Rescued.

Aouda Sobs with Relief.

Chapter 31
Fix Lends a Helping Hand

"Where is the train?" asked Phileas Fogg the moment he returned.

"Gone," said Aouda, sobbing with relief in Passepartout's arms.

"When will the next train pass through?"

"Not until this evening."

Fogg was already 20 hours behind schedule, and he had to reach New York by 9:00 in the evening on December 11 in order to catch the steamer for Liverpool.

"If you are really in such a great hurry, perhaps I can help you regain some time," offered Fix, who, at Fogg's request, had stayed to take care of Aouda at Kearney station.

"What do you have in mind, Mr. Fix?"

"There is an American named Mudge who has a sledge here—a sledge with sails! He can drive us to Omaha. There it will be easy to catch a train for New York!"

The sledge was designed to carry passengers from one station to another when heavy snow blocked the train tracks. The strong winds on the prairie could carry a sledge at a speed as fast as that of an express train.

At 8:00, the sledge was ready to start. The passengers wrapped themselves in warm traveling cloaks. The two great sails were hoisted, and the wind pushed the vehicle over the snow-covered prairie at a speed of 40 miles an hour. The distance from Fort Kearney to Omaha was about 200 miles. With luck, it could be covered in five hours.

A Sledge with Sails

Mudge had a personal interest in reaching Omaha on time, because Phileas Fogg had promised him a generous reward.

The sledge was aided by strong winds, which, however, chilled the passengers to the bone. Howling bands of prairie wolves nipped at the back of the vehicle, and Passerpartout kept his gun ready to shoot them if necessary.

Mudge reached Omaha at noon. Fogg paid him and went directly to the railroad station. A train took Fogg's party to Chicago, where another train was waiting to make the 900-mile trip to New York.

At 11:45 P.M. on December 11, Fogg, Passepartout, Aouda and Fix arrived at New York harbor. However, the *China*, one of the fastest steamers on the New York to Liverpool run, had sailed 45 minutes before.

Crossing the Prairie to Omaha by Sledge

A Carriage Ride in New York

Chapter 32
Phileas Fogg Turns Pirate

The *China* must have carried Phileas Fogg's last hope of winning his bet out to sea. But he remained as calm as ever. The travelers hired a carriage to take them to the St. Nicholas Hotel on Broadway. Phileas Fogg spent a restful night, but the others were too upset to sleep.

The next day was December 12, just nine days before Fogg's scheduled return to the Reform Club on December 21. The gentleman's entire fortune was now at stake as never before on his round-the-world voyage.

After ordering Aouda and Passepartout to be ready to leave New York at a moment's notice, Mr. Fogg left the hotel and went to the harbor. When he found a ship nearly ready to sail, he climbed aboard.

"I am Phileas Fogg, of London," he greeted the captain.

"And my name is Andrew Speedy, the captain of the *Henrietta*."

"Are you going to put to sea?"

"Yes, in an hour."

"Does your ship travel fast?"

"Her speed is 11 or 12 knots."

"That's good! Will you take me and three other people to Liverpool?"

"No, I'm going to Bordeaux, in France. Besides, I never carry passengers. They get in my way."

"Will money make a difference to you?" asked Fogg, always willing to reward generously those who performed favors for him.

Captain Speedy Never Carries Passengers.

"Money means nothing to me," replied the captain firmly.

"If you won't take me along, let me buy the *Henrietta* from you."

"No."

"Will you take me to Bordeaux, then?"

"No, not even if you pay me $200."

"I will pay you $2,000!"

"Apiece? There are four crew members."

"Apiece."

"All right," said Captain Speedy. "I will sail promptly at 9:00."

"We'll be ready," Fogg replied.

It was already 8:30. Phileas Fogg gathered up Aouda, Passepartout and Fix and brought them to the *Henrietta*. Fix's heart sank when he learned the cost of the trip. Fogg would have no money left to return to the bank when he was arrested!

$2,000 Apiece!

Captain Speedy Is Taken Prisoner.

Chapter 33
Detective Fix Springs His Trap

By the time the *Henrietta* sailed into the Atlantic Ocean, Phileas Fogg was in charge. He had bribed the crew to lock Captain Speedy in his cabin and then change the ship's course from Bordeaux to Liverpool.

There were 3,000 miles between America and England. If the weather remained good, the ocean crossing could be made easily by December 21. The engineer, however, informed "Captain" Fogg that there wasn't enough fuel to reach England!

"Feed all the fires until the coal is gone!"

Fogg ordered. Within minutes, the *Henrietta*'s smokestacks sent up great clouds of steam. On December 18, however, it became clear that the coal would be gone by nightfall.

"Bring Captain Speedy to the deck" commanded Phileas Fogg.

"Where are we?" bellowed the captain.

"We are 707 miles from Liverpool," Fogg replied very calmly.

"You are indeed a pirate!"

"I have sent for you, sir, to ask you to sell me your ship."

"No! Never!"

"But I shall have to burn her—at least her upper part. The coal has run out."

"Burn my ship? The *Henrietta* is worth 50,000 dollars!"

"Here is 60,000 dollars," said Fogg. "You see, if I don't reach London by 8:45 P.M. on December 21, I shall lose 20,000 pounds. I missed the steamer at New York, and you refused to take me to Liverpool."

The Coal Is Almost Gone.

"I made a wise decision," replied the captain, "for you have paid me handsomely for my ship!"

Phileas Fogg ordered all the wooden parts of the *Henrietta* burned. The crew tore the ship down to its flat metal hull.

On December 20, with the fires still burning, Fogg sighted the coast of Ireland. By evening, however, the steam pressure, which had been kept up by the burning wood, was about to give out completely. Mr. Fogg had less than 24 hours to reach London.

"We shall dock at Queenstown," he announced. This was the Irish port to which transatlantic steamers brought the mails. The mails were carried from the ships to Dublin, the capital of Ireland, by express trains and then sent to Liverpool by the fastest boats available. By taking the same route as the mails, Phileas Fogg could gain 12 hours over the Atlantic steamers in getting to London!

Wood for Fuel

At 1:00 in the morning, the hulk of the *Henrietta* docked at Queenstown. Fogg, Aouda, Passepartout and Detective Fix boarded the express train at once. It left the station at 1:30 and arrived in Dublin at sunrise. The travelers then caught a steamer, and on December 21 at 11:40, they sailed into Liverpool. Phileas Fogg was now only six hours away from London by train.

Suddenly, Fix pulled the warrant from his pocket, walked up to Mr. Fogg, and declared: "I arrest you in the name of the Queen of England!"

Fix Arrests Phileas Fogg.

In Prison!

Chapter 34
Back to London at Last!

Phileas Fogg was in prison! Passepartout would have strangled Fix had not some policemen held him back. He also might have blown his own brains out had his revolver been handy.

"Why didn't I tell my master what Fix was really up to?" he cried, blaming himself for the terrible mess. He had cost Phileas Fogg 20,000 pounds!

Fogg himself sat quietly in the jailhouse. As usual, he displayed no emotion. He still had almost nine hours to reach London, and the journey took only six. He laid his watch on the table and watched its hands move ever closer to the fateful hour of 8:45.

If he thought of escaping, he soon gave up the idea. The door was locked and the window heavily barred. After walking around the room, he sat down and took his diary out of his pocket. On the page for December 21, he wrote, "Liverpool, 80th day, 11:40 A.M."

The clock in the jail house struck 1:00. Fogg noticed that his watch was two hours fast.

At 2:33, Passepartout, Aouda and Detective Fix rushed into the room. Fix was out of breath, and his clothes and hair were in disarray.

"Sir," he stammered, "sir—forgive me! The bank robber was arrested three days ago! You just looked a lot like him. Now you are free!"

Phileas Fogg walked up to Fix and, with a powerful blow of his arms, knocked him flat

"Sir, Forgive Me!"

on the floor. Fogg, Aouda and Passepartout then left the jailhouse, called a taxi, and sped toward the railroad station.

It was 2:40. The express train for London had left 35 minutes ago. Phileas Fogg ordered a special train, but it was not ready until 3:00. At that hour, Mr. Fogg, having offered the engineer a generous reward for getting him to London quickly, boarded the train with Aouda and his faithful servant.

If the tracks had been clear, they could have made the trip in five and a half hours. There were delays, however, and it was 8:50 when the train reached London.

Phileas Fogg was five minutes too late. The wager was lost.

A Special Train to London

Only a Few Pounds Left

Chapter 35
A Sad Homecoming

Phileas Fogg took his bad luck in stride, but he couldn't help thinking how he had been ruined by a stupid detective after traveling around the globe, overcoming problems large and small, and braving many dangers. All that remained of the roll of banknotes he had set out with were a few pounds. The rest of his fortune—20,000 pounds—was at the bank, ready to be transferred to the gentlemen at the Reform Club. Fogg's trip cost so much money that even winning the bet would not have made him rich.

Aouda was given a room in Mr. Fogg's large house. When Passepartout reached his own room, he turned off the gas, which had been burning for 80 days. The bill from the gas company awaited him in his mailbox.

Phileas Fogg went to bed at midnight as usual, but no one knew whether he slept. The next day, for the first time in memory, he failed to leave home for the Reform Club at 11:30. In fact he spent the entire day alone in his room. Finally, at 7:30, he went downstairs for a talk with Aouda.

"Please forgive me for bringing you to England," he began. "When I took you away from India, I was rich and thought that I could put some of my wealth at your disposal. Then you would have been free and happy. Now I am ruined."

"It is *I* who should beg forgiveness, Mr. Fogg. Saving my life delayed you and thus helped to cause your ruin."

"I Am Ruined."

"But madam! You would have been killed if you had stayed in India! I had to bring you to a safe place. I still hope to put what little money I have left at your disposal."

"But what will become of you, sir?"

"I don't need anything, madam."

"Maybe your friends could help you out."

"I have no friends."

"Your relatives?"

"I no longer have any relatives."

"That really is a pity, for you have no one to confide your sorrows to." Suddenly, Aouda took Phileas Fogg's hand. "Do you want both a friend and a relative? Will you have me as your wife?"

Phileas Fogg's lips trembled, and his eyes were bright. "I love you," he said simply.

Fogg asked Passepartout to contact the Reverend Samuel Wilson at once.

"When do you wish to get married, sir?"

"Tomorrow, Monday," replied his master.

"I Love You."

Passepartout hurried to the Reverend's house. It was already past 8:00.

Making Wedding Plans

The Real Bank Robber Has Been Caught!

Chapter 36
A Good Name Restored

While Phileas Fogg was completing his trip around the world, English newspaper readers learned that the real bank robber, a Mr. James Strand, had been arrested on December 17. Suddenly Fogg, who had been wanted by the police, was an honorable gentleman once again.

A large crowd gathered around the Reform Club on Saturday evening, December 21. As the fateful hour of 8:45 neared, excitement and suspense rose to fever pitch.

At 8:20, the gentlemen with whom Fogg had made the wager gathered in the saloon.

"What time did the last train arrive from Liverpool?" asked Thomas Flanagan.

"At 7:23," replied Gautier Ralph. "The next train doesn't come until 12:10."

"If he had come on the 7:23 train, he would be here by now," said Andrew Stuart.

"Let's also remember," said John Sullivan, "that Mr. Fogg has not sent us a single message since he left, even though there are telegraph lines in all the places he visited. He is surely lost somewhere."

"There's no doubt about that," said Stuart. "The *China*, which is the only steamer Fogg could have taken from New York to arrive here on time, sailed in yesterday. His name wasn't on the passenger list."

"All that is left, then, is to present Phileas Fogg's check at the bank tomorrow," Ralph concluded.

At exactly 8:44, a roar went up from the

Making Plans to Cash Fogg's Check

crowd outside the Reform Club. The gentlemen in the saloon stopped playing whist and stood up nervously from the table. A moment later, Phileas Fogg entered the room.

"Here I am, gentlemen!" he said.

"Here I Am, Gentlemen!"

Reverend Wilson Has Startling News.

Chapter 37
A Happy Ending

Phileas Fogg won his bet after all!

He always paid an unusual amount of attention to the time but forgot that by traveling eastward, or toward the sun, he was able to gain a whole day at the end of his trip around the world.

It was Passepartout who broke the good news. He returned from Reverend Wilson's house shouting, "Master, it's impossible for you to get married tomorrow!"

"Why?"

"Tomorrow is Sunday! We arrived home 24

hours ahead of time! Tonight is Saturday, but it's already 8:40. We have only five minutes to reach the Reform Club!"

Phileas Fogg entered the club with only seconds to spare. He thus won 20,000 pounds but had spent almost 19,000 on his journey. His honor meant much more to him than money, however. He divided the remaining 1,000 pounds between Passepartout and Fix, whom he had forgiven. The servant had to pay the gas bill out of his share. That was Mr. Fogg's way of teaching him to be more careful about such things in the future.

Having settled with the gentlemen of the Reform Club, Fogg hurried home to Aouda. "Do you still wish to marry me?" he asked.

"I should ask *you* that question," she replied. "When you agreed to the wedding, you thought you were ruined. Now you are rich once again."

"Pardon me, madam, but my fortune be-

Dividing 1,000 Pounds

longs to you. If you had not suggested a wedding, Passepartout would not have gone to the Reverend Wilson's house, and I would not have found out my mistake and been able to appear on time at the Reform Club."

Phileas Fogg and Aouda were married the following day. Passepartout, who has saved the bride's life, was best man. At dawn the next morning, the servant knocked at Fogg's bedroom door.

"What brings you here so early?"

"I just wanted to tell you, sir, that we might have made the trip around the world in only 78 days."

"That's true," answered Phileas Fogg, "if we had not traveled through India. But then I would not have found Aouda!"

Passepartout closed the door and went to begin his daily chores.

Passepartout Serves the Newlyweds.

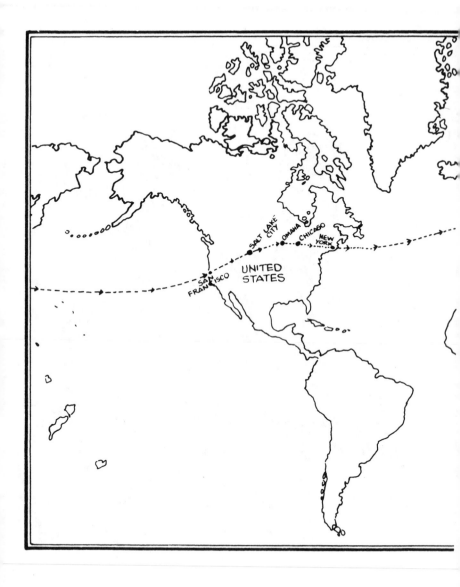

Phileas Fogg's Trip

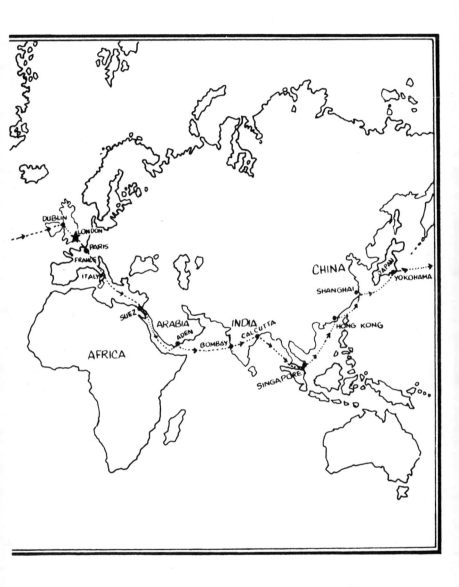

Around the World in 80 Days